D0432583

This book belongs to

_____

_____

This edition published by Parragon Books Ltd in 2015

Parragon Books Ltd
Chartist House
15–17 Trim Street
Bath BA1 1HA, UK
www.parragon.com

Copyright © 2015 Disney Enterprises, Inc.

All rights reserved. No part of this publication may be reproduced, stored in a retrieval
system or transmitted, in any form or by any means, electronic, mechanical, photocopying,
recording or otherwise, without the prior permission of the copyright holder.

ISBN 978-1-4748-0653-4

Printed in China

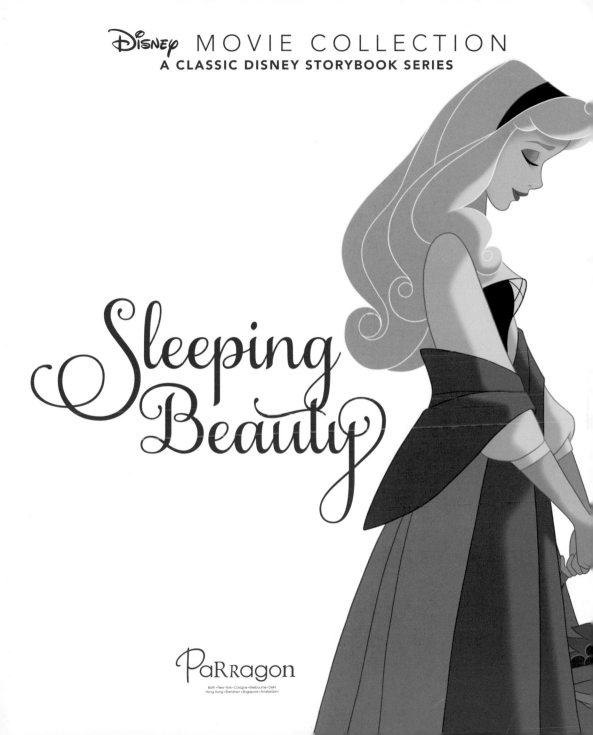

DISNEY MOVIE COLLECTION
A CLASSIC DISNEY STORYBOOK SERIES

Sleeping Beauty

PaRragon

Bath · New York · Cologne · Melbourne · Delhi
Hong Kong · Shenzhen · Singapore · Amsterdam

Once upon a time, there lived a kind king and gentle queen who wanted to have a child. After many years of hoping, they had a baby girl. They named her Aurora.

The king and queen were so happy that they held a celebration feast. Visitors came from all over the land, including King Hubert, who ruled a nearby kingdom, and his young son, Prince Phillip. The two kings decided that Phillip and Aurora would one day marry and unite the kingdoms.

During the celebration, three good fairies, Flora, Fauna and Merryweather, floated into the room. They had come to give special magical gifts to the baby princess.

"My gift shall be the gift of beauty," said Flora.

"My gift shall be the gift of song," said Fauna.

But before Merryweather could give her gift to the baby, a gust of wind blew open the doors. There was a flash of lightning, a crack of thunder and then darkness. A bright green flame appeared in the middle of the hall. It slowly took the shape of the wicked fairy Maleficent!

Maleficent was so angry about not being invited to the celebration that she put a curse on baby Aurora.

"Before the sun sets on her sixteenth birthday," she said, "she shall prick her finger on the spindle of a spinning wheel ... and die."

"Oh, no!" the queen cried.

"Seize that creature!" King Stefan, Aurora's father, ordered. But before the guards could reach Maleficent, she disappeared in a burst of fire and smoke.

Merryweather's powers were not strong enough to take away Maleficent's curse, but she was able to change it. Aurora wouldn't die – instead she would fall into a deep sleep.

Merryweather said, "From this slumber you shall wake, when true love's kiss the spell shall break."

King Stefan was so worried about Maleficent's curse that he had every spinning wheel in the kingdom burned.

But Flora came up with a better plan to protect the princess. The three fairies would transform into peasants and raise her themselves, deep in the forest. In their disguises, they would use no magic at all, so Maleficent would not be able to find them. When her sixteenth birthday had passed and the curse ended, they would return Aurora to the palace.

The king and queen wanted to do everything they could to protect Aurora, so with sadness they agreed to Flora's plan.

One night soon after, the fairies secretly slipped away with the baby princess.

Many, many years passed and high on the Forbidden Mountain, Maleficent had lost her patience. It was almost Aurora's sixteenth birthday and her evil helpers still hadn't found the princess.

"Sixteen years and not a trace of her!" Maleficent shouted. "Are you sure you've searched everywhere?"

Maleficent's last hope of finding the princess was her raven. So she ordered the bird to circle far and wide until it found a sixteen-year-old maiden with beautiful golden hair and rose-red lips.

Meanwhile, Princess Aurora had grown up to be sweet and kind. The fairies called her Briar Rose and loved her like a daughter.

On her sixteenth birthday, they sent her into the forest to pick berries and play with the animals so that they would have enough time to prepare a party for her without using magic.

Briar Rose wandered along, singing a song to her animal friends about the true love she wished for.

Nearby, a young prince heard Briar Rose's sweet singing. He urged his horse, Samson, to take him to her quickly.

Samson started galloping towards Briar Rose's singing, but when he jumped over a log, his master fell into a creek.

"No carrots for you!" scolded the prince. He got up and laid out his hat, cape and boots to dry.

When the prince wasn't looking, some of the animals borrowed his clothes. They dressed up for Briar Rose, pretending to be the prince of her dreams.

The prince began to sing along with Briar Rose.
Then they started dancing together and fell in love.
But when the prince asked her name, Briar Rose
remembered that she shouldn't speak to strangers.
But, shyly, she invited him to visit her at the cottage.

Back at the cottage, the fairies were having trouble preparing for Briar Rose's birthday party. Fauna's cake leaned to one side and the dress Flora was making didn't look right either.

The fairies had given up using magic, but now they were desperate, so they went to the attic to find something to help them.

Sure that no one would see them, the fairies made everything perfect – with help from their magic wands.

But while Flora and Merryweather were arguing about the colour of Briar Rose's dress, they accidentally let their magic escape up the chimney.

Just as Maleficent's raven was flying overhead searching for Aurora, colourful sparkles from the magic wands shot out of the cottage's chimney.

The raven flew back to the Forbidden Mountain quickly to tell Maleficent that it had found the good fairies – and the princess!

When Briar Rose returned home, she was delighted with her birthday surprises.

She then told the fairies all about the handsome stranger she'd met, and they knew that it was time to tell Briar Rose the truth.

They explained that Briar Rose was actually the
Princess Aurora and was promised to marry Prince Phillip.

Aurora cried and cried because this meant she couldn't
marry the young man she had met in the forest. Little did
she know the young man *was* Prince Phillip!

The fairies set off to return the princess to the castle and
her parents, the king and queen.

When they reached the palace, the fairies left Aurora alone while they went to find her parents. Suddenly a strange glow appeared in front of the princess. In a trance, she followed the light up a winding staircase.

The long staircase led to a secret room with
a spinning wheel in it. When Aurora stepped inside,
Maleficent appeared and commanded her to touch
the spindle.

Powerless against the evil fairy's magic, the princess
obeyed Maleficent and pricked her finger on the spindle's
sharp point.

Meanwhile, the good fairies returned to the hall and saw that Aurora had gone. They followed the stairway to the secret room. There they found Maleficent standing over the fallen princess.

Sadly, the three fairies took Aurora up to a tower room where they placed her gently on a bed with a rose in her hand. Tears ran down the fairies' cheeks at this cruel turn of events.

Merryweather, Fauna and Flora were very worried that the king and queen would find Aurora, so they decided to put everyone else at the palace into a deep sleep until they could undo Maleficent's curse.

King Hubert was visiting the palace that night. As he was falling asleep, Flora heard him say that Prince Phillip wanted to marry a peasant girl.

"Briar Rose!" Flora cried. She quickly found the other fairies and they rushed to meet Prince Phillip at the cottage.

Meanwhile, Phillip and Samson had arrived at the cottage, as arranged. Inside, Maleficent and her evil creatures were waiting, ready to trap him. She knew that the brave prince was the only person who could undo her curse on Aurora, so Maleficent had to keep him away from the princess.

Maleficent took the prince back to her castle and locked him in her dungeon. She revealed to him that the peasant girl was Princess Aurora and that only his kiss could awaken her. Phillip knew he had to escape to save his true love.

Just then, the good fairies appeared. They freed Prince Phillip quickly and gave him the magical Shield of Virtue and Sword of Truth.

"These weapons of righteousness will triumph over evil," they told him.

As the good fairies and Phillip were leaving
the dungeon, Maleficent's raven spotted them.
    The black bird quickly told its wicked mistress
that the prince had escaped.

To keep the prince away from Aurora,
Maleficent conjured a wall of thorns around him.
Using the Sword of Truth, Phillip quickly cut a path
through the branches and rode away on Samson.

As the prince approached the castle's bridge,
Maleficent turned herself into a terrifying dragon
and blasted him with red-hot flames. Phillip used
the Shield of Virtue to protect himself and Samson.

The good fairies saw that Prince Phillip was in danger, so they sprinkled his sword with fairy dust. "Now, Sword of Truth, fly swift and sure, that evil die and good endure," they said.

Then the prince threw his sword at the dragon with all his might. The beast fell back and plunged over the edge of the cliff!

Prince Phillip ran through the palace gates and
up to the tower where Aurora lay. He knelt beside the
princess and kissed her gently on the lips.

The Sleeping Beauty awakened and smiled happily
at her true love.

Before long, everyone else in the kingdom awoke, too, including King Stefan and the queen. The princess and her parents hugged joyfully, happy to be reunited at last.

Soon after, Princess Aurora married Prince Phillip and they lived happily ever after.